For Abigail and Elise

with love from

Karen

12—

Jacques' Jungle Ballet

Written by Karen Lavut   Illustrated by Nicola Rigg

Aurum Books for Children
London

Once upon a time there was a young
elephant who lived in the jungle with his
family and all the other wild animals.
His name was Jacques. Jacques enjoyed
clomping through the forest with his
brothers and sisters, pulling leaves off the
trees to eat, spraying himself in the pond
and resting in the shade at mid-day. But
he was not completely satisfied.

Jacques wanted to be a ballet dancer.

His parents were baffled. They had no idea how Jacques could have ever seen, or even heard of, the ballet. They told him to get that silly idea right out of his head. They told him that elephants were meant to be elephants, not dancers.

'I won't have a son of mine turning into a ballet dancer!' shouted his father angrily.

'He'll grow out of it, dear,' said his mother, soothingly.

But Jacques did not grow out of it. He was determined. He would be a ballet dancer.

The other animals laughed at him. His brothers and sisters wouldn't play with him anymore. Jacques was left all alone.

To forget his loneliness, Jacques practised. He taught himself how to dance by watching. He hid behind a tree and watched the impalas leap. He watched the cheetahs, panthers, leopards, lions and tigers stalking their prey. He watched the monkeys swinging from branch to branch. He watched the frogs in the pond and the hummingbirds hovering above.

Jacques had to work very hard because elephants are so big and heavy. He learned to pirouette like a spinning stone. He learned to criss-cross his feet like beating wings. He learned to stand with his trunk stretched out in front and his tail stretched out behind.

After 10 years Jacques was finally ready. He decided to give the animals a concert. He imagined how excited they would be.

'Bravo Jacques!' they would shout.

'I'm proud of you, my boy!' his father would say.

But nobody came to the concert. Jacques was heartbroken.

He decided to leave the jungle and seek his fortune far away.

Jacques walked for three days until his path was blocked by a river. The river was full of crocodiles. But Jacques swam across. Every time a crocodile came near him he gave a terrific kick. His legs were very strong from his training.

He walked and walked until there were no more trees and no more grass – only sand. He nearly died of thirst. But he staggered on until at last he came to a mountain.

Slowly and painfully, Jacques climbed the mountain. When he got to the top he could see a city.

'There are thousands of people in a city!' said Jacques to himself. 'They'll know all about ballet. They'll understand why I want to dance!'

The city was noisy and confusing. Traffic sped past. There were many buildings and few trees. Jacques went up to one of the people on the street.

'Excuse me, is there a ballet company
in this city?'
  The stranger noticed that Jacques was
an elephant but, being polite, she did not
comment. She took him to the Ballet
Theatre. Jacques thanked her with a bow.

Jacques knocked on the stage-door. It was opened by the manager who said rudely, 'What do you want?'

'Good morning, sir. I'm a ballet dancer. I would like to dance with your company,' said Jacques.

'You're not a ballet dancer – you're an elephant! Get out!'

'But sir, I've come all the way from the jungle . . .'

'Then go back to the jungle, that's where you belong!'

And he slammed the door in Jacques' face.

The next morning, Jacques was back.

'You again!' said the manager.

'I may be an elephant, but I'm also a dancer,' said Jacques.

'Out! Out! Out!' screamed the manager so loudly that the director came rushing to the door. He was surprised to find the manager shouting at an elephant.

'What's going on here?' he asked. The director's name was Basil. He smiled at Jacques and said, 'What can I do for you?'

'Please let me dance in your company,' said Jacques.

'But you're an elephant . . .'

'I'm a dancer! I'm good, I'm really good!'

'That doesn't matter – you're still an elephant. Elephants are very nice, they aren't meant for the stage, that's all. You're too big and heavy.'

Jacques sank his head on to his chest. A tear trickled down his cheek.

Basil didn't know what to do. He felt sorry for Jacques, but he was in the middle of a dress rehearsal. 'Here's a free ticket for tonight's show. I'm sure you'll enjoy it. Goodbye, now, and good luck.'

By evening, hundreds of people were standing outside the theatre, waiting to buy tickets. Jacques handed his ticket to an usher. 'I'm sorry, sir, but you are too big for the seat. Would you mind standing at the back?'

He had an excellent view. The place was as crowded as the jungle. The audience was talking softly, not like the chattering and shrieking he was used to. There was a delicate smell of perfume – though not as strong as the jungle smell of earth and flowers. Then he heard the orchestra tuning up – that sounded like the jungle!

The lights dimmed slowly until it was dark. There was quiet.
A spotlight shone on a man who bowed, then faced the orchestra
and raised his hands. He was the conductor! And then there was
the most wonderful music Jacques had ever heard.

Slowly the curtain rose.

When the ballet was over, the audience applauded wildly and
threw flowers on to the stage. But Jacques couldn't move. He was
spellbound. Tears of joy stood in his eyes.

Jacques was at the ballet again the next night. And the next.
He came every night for a whole week.

At the end of the week Jacques was at the stage-door again.

'Oh dear,' sighed Basil.

Without wasting another word, Jacques did a pirouette and an arabesque.

'Extraordinary!' gasped Basil. 'But you're the wrong shape. I'm terribly sorry. Why don't you try the circus?'

So that's what Jacques did.

He found the circus tent in a big park. 'Excuse me!' he called.

A woman came out of the tent. Her name was Monica, and she was the owner. 'Yes?' she snapped.

'Good afternoon, madam. I am a ballet dancer and . . .'

'A ballet dancer? Don't make me laugh! It takes a year to get a brute like you to stand on two legs – never mind dance! Ha, ha! Tell me another!'

Jacques was learning fast that words were useless. He made a running leap and did a triple turn in the air.

'Well, well, well!' said Monica. 'Why didn't you say so? I think we can use you – when can you start?'

'Right now,' said Jacques.

In the evening Jacques saw hundreds of people filing into the Big Top. He heard a band playing. He saw animals being led into the tent, and clowns running behind them. Then came the jugglers, acrobats and trapeze artists.

At long last Monica came for Jacques. 'You'll need dressing up.' She tied a red velvet sash around Jacques' waist and a bunch of purple feathers behind each ear. Then she led Jacques to the entrance. 'Now's your big moment,' she said. 'You'd better be good. Ladies and gentlemen! We are proud to present the greatest ballet dancer on earth – Jacques, the elephant!'

A fanfare of trumpets and drums announced Jacques' entrance.
Never had he seen such a crowd! The lights were dazzling.
Jacques ran lightly round the ring. He lifted three legs off the
ground and stood on the toes of one foot. The spectators went
wild. They clapped, stamped their feet, whistled and cheered until
their voices were hoarse. They made so much noise throughout
his dance that Jacques couldn't hear the music. He gave 32 curtain
calls, but they wouldn't let him go. People poured into the ring
from all sides. If he hadn't been an elephant, he might have been
crushed to death.

Jacques became famous overnight. Tons of flowers were delivered to him. People flocked to see him. He was written about in the newspapers and talked about on the radio. He was on television. A red carpet was laid from his trailer to the Big Top. Hundreds of people were turned away from his shows. Monica became a millionaire.

But Jacques wasn't happy.

The crowds gave him no privacy. They followed him everywhere. He longed for a quiet place to hide in peace. But Monica wouldn't let Jacques out of her sight.

Jacques didn't even enjoy doing his act. The loud music hurt his ears. It sounded ugly after the beautiful ballet music. The silly feathers and ridiculous sashes he had to wear embarrassed him. Monica made him perform sensational feats all the time. Jacques didn't want to show off in stupid costumes to flashy music. He wanted to dance – gracefully, superbly, sublimely – like a real ballet dancer.

He decided to leave the circus.

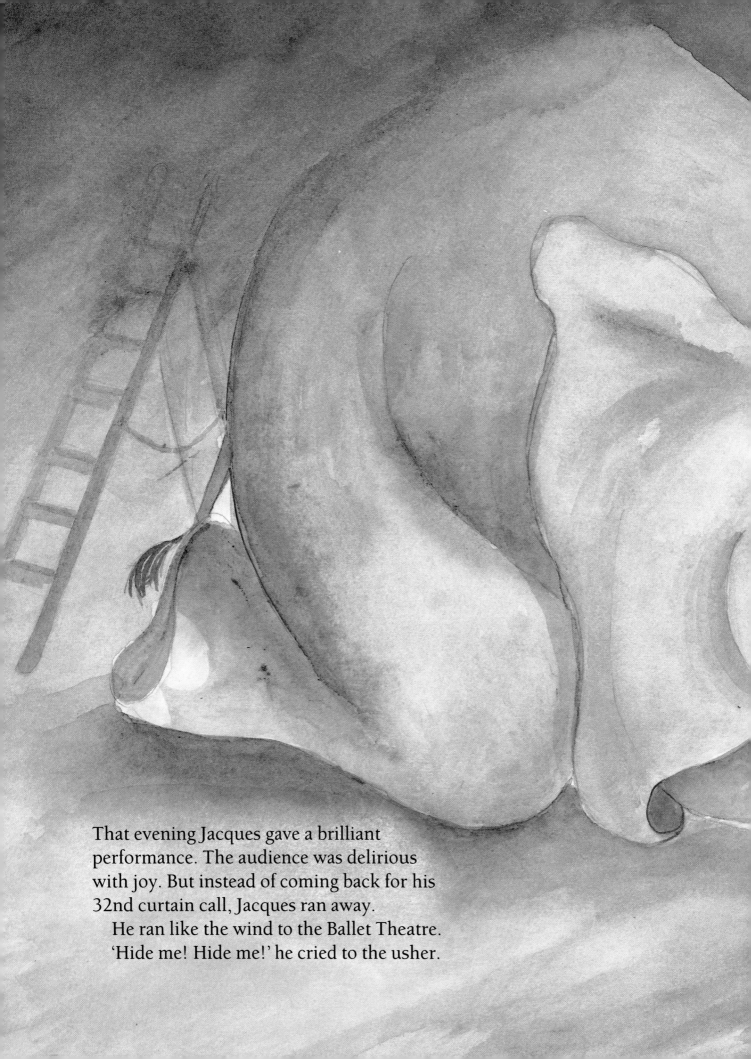

That evening Jacques gave a brilliant
performance. The audience was delirious
with joy. But instead of coming back for his
32nd curtain call, Jacques ran away.
  He ran like the wind to the Ballet Theatre.
  'Hide me! Hide me!' he cried to the usher.

The performance had just come to an end, and the audience was making a lot of noise clapping and cheering. Jacques followed the usher to a storage room under the stage.

It was pitch dark inside. Jacques could hear the dancers' feet going pitter-patter on the stage above his head, and the roar of applause. Then the sounds died away and Jacques waited in the dark. He waited the whole night.

Early the next morning the dancers' feet were going pitter-patter again. But nobody came for Jacques. He knocked on the ceiling with his trunk. Thump! Thump! Thump!

The dancers opened the trap door and out stepped Jacques. Basil came from the wings. 'What are you doing here?' he asked.

'I hate the circus, please let me join your company!'

'But you're an ele–'

'So what? I can dance!'

'Tell you what,' Basil said brightly, 'you can teach. You can teach my dancers everything that you know. You can teach them to dance like you!'

Suddenly the orchestra began to play. Jacques could not resist. He began to dance. He danced as he had never danced before. The others crept back to watch. As the last note faded, the prima ballerina threw herself at Jacques and cried, 'Teach me!

Jacques taught the Ballet Theatre everything he had learned in the jungle. He taught them how to beat their feet in the air like the wings of a hummingbird. He taught them how to leap like an impala. He taught them how to stand still as a statue on one foot, like a flamingo.

He was demanding. Nothing less than perfect would do.
'No, no! Pretend you're a panther: one, two, three, leap!'
In time the dancers became almost as good as Jacques. The
Ballet Theatre was now the best in the world, and Jacques was
as famous a teacher as he was a dancer.

But there was something missing in Jacques' life. He was not
dancing. He had to dance.

   He began to dream of the jungle. At least in the jungle he'd been
able to dance to his heart's content.

   He would go back to the jungle.

   The dancers cried. The musicians cried. Basil cried. 'What will
we do without you, Jacques?' he asked, clasping his trunk. 'We'll
never forget you!'

   Jacques cried too. He kissed everyone.

Jacques went home the way he had come.
Over the mountain. Through the desert.
Across the river. At last he arrived in the
jungle.

'I suppose the animals will poke fun at me
again,' he said to himself.

But word of his fame had reached even
the jungle. The birds were the first to
recognise him. They flew ahead, spreading
the news, 'Jacques is back! Jacques is back!'

The animals came running and leaping, creeping and crawling to greet Jacques, the world-famous dancer. Four hippopotami hoisted Jacques on to their shoulders and everybody cheered. His mother and father were very proud.

'I told you he'd make good,' said his mother.

His father remembered what she had really said. But he didn't remind her.

They gave Jacques a magnificent party.

Soon Jacques was dancing again. He practised for hours every day while the animals watched respectfully.

One day an impala started to dance with him. Soon a giraffe joined in. It gave Jacques an idea: he would form his own ballet company! All the animals were invited to join, no matter how fat or how big or how small or how ugly. No one was left out. There were places for the elephants, the hippopotami, the giraffes, the lions, the tigers, the leopards, the panthers, the cheetahs, the impalas, the monkeys, the birds, the frogs, the snakes, the dragonflies, the butterflies, the bees and the spiders.

The music was composed and played by the birds, frogs, crickets, bees and mosquitos.

Jacques was teacher, choreographer and principal dancer. They practised in the mornings, rehearsed in the afternoons and performed in the evenings. There was a show every night, and two on Saturdays.

Jacques danced until he was 85. And for many years after that, he could be seen, night after night, sitting in the front row, watching his Jungle Ballet.

For Kate and Marinda KL
For George and John NR

Text © 1989 Karen Lavut
Illustrations © 1989 Nicola Rigg

First published 1989 by Aurum Books for Children
33 Museum Street, London WC1A 1LD

Printed and bound in Hong Kong

British Library Cataloguing in Publication Data

Lavut, Karen
Jacques' jungle ballet
I. Title II. Rigg, Nicola
823'.54 [J]

ISBN 1–85406–018–X